The
of Adu

C000148842

by Mistress Jade
(with Mark Maguire)

Published by
markmaguirebooks.co.uk

The Benefits of Adult Discipline

by Mistress Jade
(with Mark Maguire)

In "Paying with Pain", read what happens to swarthy hunk Nick, 37, when his angry partner Amanda decides to punish him for running up a huge credit card bill that he just can't hope to pay off.

Amanda, busty, buxom at just 19, has just started work as a receptionist in a big hotel, while Nick, older, more mature and experienced, is well suited for his work in an office.

When Amanda discovers Nick' overspending, they visit a lifestyle shop together to find a means of teaching Nick a lesson he won't forget. Nick has to take a crook-handled whippy cane up to the counter and pay for it out of his own money, with the pretty young assistant knowing it's soon going to be in use across Nick's bare buttocks. For Amanda, Nick's humiliation is just as important as the pain, and she makes sure her older, handsome partner experiences a good dose of both!

By chance, while buying the cane together, they meet their friend Jennifer who, at 61 years old and sister of an ex public schoolboy, knows from plenty of personal experience, just how effective regular canings can be in modifying recalcitrant young men's behaviour.

Enjoy really detailed descriptions of the imaginative punishments Nick submits to. Discover how he writhes and squirms under the relentless rhythm of numerous painful cane strokes applied again and again by his younger partner Amanda, while their friend Jennifer watches and offers advice. Jennifer demonstrates how Amanda can learn to apply good, painful cane strokes HARD, right across the lower parts of her older partner's arse, which she soon discovers is the most sensitive area of all.

Try to imagine just how humiliating – and horny – it would be to submit in the ways

Nick grows to dread, then to love, and eventually enjoy!

Then read an EXTRA bonus story, "Taking it HARD!"

Jonathan and Emily meet at a hotel conference, where Emily introduces Jonathan to the delights of the cane in her hotel executive suite.

All the characters in both stories are horny as hell, and all of them are connected in the different ways you'll read about, as each one comes to understand and appreciate the many benefits of consensual adult corporal punishment.

Paying with Pain

The letter that dropped on the mat changed everything.

It had been a pleasant Saturday morning for Amanda and Nick. Amanda, 29, and Nick, 37, had been together for two and a half years, living in a small flat near Vauxhall Station, south London. They had a pretty good relationship, all things considered. Nick, swarthy hunk, masculine and "hung" always liked plenty of bedroom action, and Amanda had no complaints at all about that! Slim, curvy, and equally keen on "adult relations", she could easily take everything that Nick could give. On a Saturday morning, they usually woke late, showered, and then got down to a hot, horny session that could often take up half the morning.

Not this particular Saturday.

The letter contained the joint credit card bill the two of them received every month. Normally about a grand altogether, they always paid off half of it each, funds coming from each of their own separate bank accounts. This bill was different. Printed at the top, in big red letters, was WARNING! LIMIT EXCEEDED.

The balance due was £3405.53, and their credit limit was £3000.

The couple never went anywhere near their limit. They always paid off the amount due every month, so they never had to pay any of the high interest charges they would incur if they left anything owing.

"What the fuck?" Amanda was incredulous.

Blushing, and looking rather sheepish, Nick hurriedly put on his boxers, commenting "I'll go and make some coffee".

Amanda responded right away. "You'll stay right here", she ordered. "You know about this, don't you?"

"I'm really sorry, darling", Nick said quietly. "I got into a betting site on line, and it all just got a bit out of hand. You could easily add more money, and I kept thinking if I put just a bit more in, I'd be bound to win eventually."

"But you didn't win, did you?" Amanda retorted. "You didn't win anything, and we've both LOST more than three grand. We can't pay this. You know we can't. We haven't got that sort of cash."

Nick for once was silent.

"And it doesn't end there, does it? If we don't pay, they add interest at 39%! Thirty nine percent! That's more than a third! You've got to be kidding, man. And I tell you what. You've got to be punished."

Nick blushed bright red as he heard his partner say this. What kind of punishment did she have in mind? The whole morning had changed beyond all recognition. Thoughts of a nice, slow, leisurely fuck had completely vanished, and were now replaced with the idea of his younger partner disciplining him in some way.

"What do you mean? What are you going to do?" he asked, gingerly.

"I remember my dad telling me one time that he'd stolen some money when he was young. He got the cane."

The word brought about an immediate change in Nick. He blushed bright red and eventually managed to whisper,

"Cane?"

"Yes. Six of the best. You always got six strokes, Dad said, and they were always applied to your BARE bum."

Further embarrassed silence followed, until Nick managed to speak.

"Yes, but that was then and this is now", Nick ventured, highly embarrassed that his partner had mentioned such a famously painful and completely humiliating punishment.

Amanda was warming to her subject.

"We'll do this together, like we always do everything. We'll pay off the balance as much as we can each month until it's gone."

Nick ran across the room and hugged his beautiful young partner. "Thanks", he said. "I love you. You know that."

"And I love you", came the reply. "That's why I'm going to teach you a very worthwhile lesson. A very PAINFUL lesson, in fact. Just like my dad, you're going to get the cane, and I'm going to cane you every week until the credit card balance is down to zero."

"You can't be serious!"

"Oh yes, I'm very serious. You and I have both seen the canes in the LifeStyle shop at Earls Court. They always have a certain fascination for me. Just the sight of them does something to me. Well, I'm sure one of those slim, flexible beauties will be very effective when put to practical use across a gorgeous, hairy arse like yours."

"The cane was always for the young. Young men only. And only when they were students at college. It's not appropriate for a guy of 37."

"I think you and I both know it's going to hurt you just as much as anyone else.

Whether you're 18 or 80. Your buttocks are soft, a cane is thin and flexible, and it's going to absolutely burn and STING like hell, whatever your age."

After a few more minutes of increasingly fractious argument, Amanda suddenly declared,

"OK. It's over, Nick. I'm done with you. If you don't take the discipline I'm offering, I'm out of this relationship. I love you. You know that. So, I'm offering to do this BECAUSE I love you. And you'll accept the discipline out of love for me. It'll do you the world of good."

Put like that, the caning sounded like a gift. How could Nick refuse? But that missed the point. Just how painful was it going to be?

Before Nick could ask for more detail about what his younger partner was proposing, Amanda continued.

Don't worry. This punishment regime is going to be organized on a very loving basis."

Laughing to herself, she went on, "Loving! That's right. It's going to be loving because I'M going to be loving it!"

Nick suddenly realised his partner was serious. If he didn't submit to what she was proposing, he'd lose her for good. What would he rather have? A sore backside and a loving, devoted Other Half? Or keep his pride – alone?

That was the nub of it, though. His pride. How could he possibly bare his bum, bend over and meekly present it for regular canings from a pretty young woman? How could he possibly agree to be so humiliated? But that was what young men at the colleges of old had to do (admittedly not for a woman) and, when asked, you always heard them say it never did them any harm at all. In fact, Nick had heard several old men say the canings they'd had were the making of them. Suddenly he blurted out,

"I'll do it!"

Nick couldn't believe what he'd just said, but now he'd said it.

"You're going to submit to my punishments?"

"Yes."

"It'll be VERY painful."

"I know."

"And unbelievably humiliating. Embarrassment is hardly going to be the word for what I've got in mind."

"What?"

"I think weekly, hard canings should be the basis of what we agree to do together - until the credit card balance is paid off – and I've got a few ideas that could definitely ENHANCE your discipline regime." Amanda grinned from ear to ear as she spoke.

"What sort of things?"

"Oh, that's for you to wonder and only me to know!"

As soon as this remark was made, the situation changed. Nick felt a real stirring in his loins. His cock started to swell as he took in what he'd just agreed to. He, at 37, was going to submit to his younger partner every Friday evening. Something told him the pain might be worth it, if the whole thing turned him on as much as he was beginning to think it would!

Without any more discussion, the two lovers got dressed, had their usual Saturday breakfast of croissants and coffee, and then stepped out into the street together. A short walk to Vauxhall Station, a change at Clapham Junction, and they were on their way to West Brompton where they would be just in time for the Saturday morning opening of LifeStyle at 11 am.

The store contained a wide assortment of items, all of interest. Clothing, underwear, greetings cards, DVDs, calendars, poppers, and towards the back of the shop, a selection of canes. Whippy, flexible, crook handled, they were all the "real thing", capable of causing an intense sting upon landing across adult male buttocks, and leaving clear red stripes in their wake.

The two partners started to rifle through the selection. Some were a little longer, some were a little thicker, all had the iconic curved handle. They'd only just begun looking when the attractive young sales assistant approached them. She was slim, smart, still in her twenties.

"You alright there guys?"

Amanda responded. "Just looking at the canes."

"Yes, we've got a very good selection. And they're quite popular for those who want to play discipline games. Or, of course, if you want to punish a guy for real. Has he been misbehaving?"

Nick froze, and blushed bright red.

"Well, go on, tell him!" Amanda prompted.

"Yes, I guess." Nick ventured. That was all he could manage to say.

The young assistant grinned. "Turn around", she commanded. "Let's have a look at your arse."

Nick couldn't believe the situation he was in. Reluctantly he swivelled round a bit, while the young woman continued "36-inch waist? Nice full cheeks. Any one of our canes will make an excellent impression on those two beauties."

Nick felt his cock stirring as the young assistant enquired, "Hairy or smooth?"

Amanda, now grinning also, came back with "Hairy. My favourite kind."

"Agreed", replied the assistant. "Like I say, any of these canes will make a guy's bare bum bounce, whether it's smooth or hairy."

Amanda was becoming more enthusiastic by the minute. "Great", she replied. "Can you help us choose a good one? My other half here knows he deserves to be punished, and I'm determined to do it properly. This not for playing any discipline games."

The young assistant was only too pleased to help. "I think medium length is good, to land across both cheeks, and medium thickness definitely hurts the most. I guess that's what you're looking for if this real punishment."

She handed Amanda a nice example for her to feel.

Amanda ran her hand up and down its slender length. "Mmmmm. Feels good. A bit whippy, but not too much."

"That's what you want. To control it you need to be accurate, and you can't be accurate if it's too thin and flailing about all over the place."

"Right. We'll take this one. Nick is paying for it, out of his own money. That way I think he'll appreciate the value of what we've bought."

Nick, virtually quivering with embarrassment, carried the instrument of his forthcoming discipline to the counter. Just as he put the cane down on the counter, they heard a voice.

"Well! What have we here? Somebody's been naughty!"

They all turned around to see an older, much older, very smartly dressed woman. It was their friend Jennifer. Immaculately turned out in matching skirt and top, white blouse and pretty, floral scarf, Jennifer was well preserved, even though she was now in her early sixties.

As the sister of an ex public schoolboy, Jennifer knew only too well, just how much the cane could hurt. Her brother had told her as much, many times. Nevertheless, she always maintained that the best way to uphold discipline, manners and general good behaviour was to make any miscreant submit to a good, hard caning as an excellent reminder to always toe the line.

Nowadays, Jennifer also loved discussing the subject of corporal punishment. Her brother's experiences bent across the headmaster's desk several decades earlier had given her a real taste for stories of the cane and indeed, on more than a few occasions, she'd indulged in adult discipline games where she was always the "mistress" and a selection of very handsome men were the victims.

A very horny discussion ensued, during which Amanda explained Nick's financial crimes and what they were going to do about it. Jennifer agreed with the assistant that the medium thickness cane would be the best one. She was able to make the same points, that accuracy would be maintained if it wasn't too whippy, while the medium thickness would ensure it would hurt as much as possible. All the while, Nick hopped from foot to foot in complete humiliation.

Eventually Jennifer asked "When is the first caning taking place? Only I'd like to be there. I always enjoy watching a discipline session, and I might be able to help. I could give you some advice, and I could give Nick a few strokes myself, to show you how best to do it. I'm not exactly inexperienced when it comes to that sort of thing! Maybe you didn't know that?"

Amanda was delighted. If truth be told, the extra enhancements she'd mentioned when discussing the forthcoming punishments with Nick earlier were based around the idea of getting an audience to watch. Nick was beside himself with embarrassment. Nevertheless, the deal was done. Jennifer would join the couple at their home on the following Friday at 7 pm for Nick's introduction to the many benefits of caning!

* * * * * * * *
* * *

There we find the three of them. Two with a glass of nicely chilled pino grigio, and one bending over the kitchen table. How well his masculine buttocks fill his tight, thin trousers, and how appealing his bum cheeks look as he nervously bends over for a really good, hard caning from his loving partner. The first of many that would gradually pay for his silly mistake with the credit card.

Nick had dressed as instructed. Black trousers, thin, white cotton briefs underneath. Briefs that would be revealed when his trousers came down after the first six strokes, and briefs that themselves would be pulled down after Nick' second six swipes, to expose his hairy cheeks for the final, hardest six.

"Why don't you start things off?" Amanda suggested, handing the cane to Jennifer.

"Certainly", she replied. "Raise your bum, young man, and we'll begin. Remember to keep still, keep your arse up nice and high, and your legs as far apart as they'll go."

Nick did his best comply. Once Jennifer was satisfied with his position, the waiting game began. She took a few more leisurely sips of her dry white wine.

"One of the aspects of corporal punishment that's often forgotten is anticipation", she explained. "The position itself is very humiliating, and the humiliation is only compounded by making the guy WAIT. Just tap his bum very lightly, draw the cane across both buttocks slowly, tease him, tap him, stroke him. He'll get more and more anxious until he actually WANTS the stroke."

Jennifer spent several minutes demonstrating this technique, then ...

THWHACK!

The first stroke was a beauty. Right across the centre of Nick' proffered cheeks.

THWHACK! THWHACK! Two more in fairly quick succession. Both a little lower down.

Nick jumped at every stroke, his legs stretched further, and his hands gripped the far edge of the table so hard that he was literally clinging on for dear life.

THWHACK!   Another one. Now the strokes were producing a vocal response.

"Aaaaaaaah, owwwww! No!"

THWHACK!

Nick was covered in sweat, breathing in and out in short, shallow gasps. Nothing could have prepared him for this. He could never in his wildest dreams have imagined that it would hurt this much!

Jennifer walked round to the front of the table, flexing the cane near to Nick' face. "Why are you being caned, Nick?"

"For overspending, Miss."

Everyone stopped short. Nick had just called Jennifer "Miss"!

Was he really getting into the whole scene?

Jennifer now spoke just like her brother's headmaster had done all those years ago.

"I told you this behaviour would not be tolerated, did I not?"

Nick swallowed and spoke again, still almost whispering, "Yes Miss, you did."

"Well, now you're feeling the consequences of your actions, aren't you? Am I making an impression on you, young man? Well?"

"Yes, Miss. You are, Miss. Definitely, Miss. A very definite impression, Miss!"

There was almost an air of cheekiness creeping into Nick' responses. The caning was certainly having an effect – and not an unusual effect for a man in his prime like Nick.

"Well, let us reinforce it shall we? Next two strokes. Keep in position, bottom up."

Nick stretched over the desk again, resigned to what was happening, but now beginning to appreciate the hot, deep, burning sensation that was engulfing his nether regions. Amanda was mesmerised. She hadn't expected her older partner to respond in such a positive, encouraging way.

THWHACK!

Without any warning, the fifth stroke landed, even lower, right across the crease where Nick' buttocks met the top of his legs. Now that DID hurt!

"Aaaaaaaaaaargh ... Owwwwww ... No! ... Please! ... No! ... Owwwwwwwwwww!!"

Jennifer spoke clearly. "What do you mean 'No'? You've agreed to this. Remember?"

THWHACK!

While Nick was still gasping, shouting, and trying to cope with the fifth stroke, the sixth was delivered with real technique. A really hard swipe, it cut right across the same area that the previous stroke had hit.

Nick clung to the edge of the table. His knuckles were almost white, his face was bright red, and contorted in pain.

"Aaaaaaaargh! … AAAAAAAAARGH! … OWWWWWWW!"

He jumped to his feet, frantically rubbing his blazing buttocks in a futile attempt to rub out the burning, throbbing pain. He hopped about, dancing from foot to foot, while the two women watched, fascinated. Despite the raging pain, Nick's cock was really hard now, inside her pants.

Eventually, Jennifer spoke. "I'm glad you're on your feet, as we need your trousers to come down now, for the second part of your punishment. The second of three parts. Pull your trousers down, step out of them and place them neatly on the chair. Then bend over again for your next six strokes which will be delivered just across your underpants, and as you may have guessed, will also be applied a LITTLE harder."

Nick took in all Jennifer had just said. It was the way she said it that was so humiliating. The calmness belied the devastating effect the caning was having. Nevertheless, Nick struggled out of his trousers while the two watched, sipping their wine, and then placed himself back in position, stretched across the table, bottom attractively raised, now just protected by his thin white cotton briefs.

Jennifer handed the cane to Amanda. "All yours," she said. "Remember accuracy is the whole thing. Apply the strokes low down, and try to punish both buttocks equally."

Amanda tapped the cane on her partner's well-presented bum. Nick tensed up, anticipating that every new stroke would necessarily have to be across the area punished before, on top of the welts already rising on his arse. Amanda wasn't going to be in any hurry. Copying the technique that Jennifer had demonstrated so well, she spent quite a while gently tapping the tip of the cane onto different parts of her older partner's arse. She then followed with light rubbing of both buttocks with one hand, while stroking the length of the slender cane with the other hand.

Tap, tap, tap. Then ... THWHACK!

"AAAAAAAARRRRRRRGGGGGGGHHHHH!"

 That one was so hard, no pause for Nick to think when it might be coming, just a good, lusty stroke searing across his already striped bum.

"BE QUIET, OR YOU WILL GET ANOTHER SIX, ARE WE CLEAR?"

"Y-e-s, Miss".

From somewhere, deep inside, a resolve spread through Nick. I can do this. I am a man. I know I deserve it, so I'm going to get through it without any fuss. Something more urgent came to him. A feeling that was growing more and more intense. I..... I need it. I....want it. His cock was even harder now, pressing into the surface of the table, desperately needing relief.

He gritted his teeth, gripped the desk, straightened his legs, and raised up his arse. A gesture that was saying "Give it to me!" and "I can take whatever you can give."

THWHACK!

A strangled gasp of a response.

THWHACK!

Nick gritted his teeth harder.

THWHACK!

His head rose up, neck stretched back.

THWHACK!

Straining every sinew.

The fifth stroke was another beauty, applied harder, really low down. Only one more stroke to go. Amanda spoke this time.

"You're doing well, my love. Just one more of this set of six, and you will probably be able to guess what kind of a stroke it's going to be."

Silence.

"Can you guess?"

"A harder stroke," came the whispered reply.

"Exactly! Bottom up, legs spread apart, nice and straight."

Tap, tap, tap, then ...

THWHACK!

Panting, sweating, and still gasping, Nick stayed in position, presenting his caned arse towards the two women standing behind him, waiting until he was told to stand up. He could feel his cock twitching, straining, rampant.

"Right young man, well done, stand up."

Amanda passed the cane to Jennifer.

"I think you'd better give him the final six," she said. "I'm not sure if I can do them accurately enough. I know you said they'd need to be quite a lot harder, and I'm likely to go a bit off target if I cane hard enough to have the right effect."

Jennifer grinned, and took the excellent instrument of punishment. Stroking its length, she said ...

"Pants down, get in position, face down of course."

Still smarting from the thrashing, and now resigned to his fate, Nick pushed his pants down to his ankles and stepped out of them. As he stretched across the table once more, the two women could admire their handiwork so far. His firm, masculine cheeks were both adorned with twelve beautiful stripes that burned and throbbed bright red. Now all that remained, for today at least, was to add ANOTHER six, to complete the picture.

Jennifer tapped Nick' bare bum twice, and everyone in the room knew they were now at the point of no return. Nick didn't know how he would react. He had never had a proper caning before. Would he be able to take it? Would he jump up and grab his backside, meriting extra strokes? Would he disgrace himself by whimpering and pleading? Would he let himself down at the last minute?

Jennifer, now swishing the cane menacingly through the air, was enjoying the view before her. She was in no hurry to proceed, having already explained that anticipation is part of the torment of a proper caning. As a result, Nick' nervousness increased.

There was a pregnant pause and then Jennifer spoke, with a clear, public school kind of a voice.

"Do you understand why you are being punished?"

"Yes Miss."

"Very well. We all agreed upon a thorough caning for you, but I think a delay to the last part of your caning might be helpful. I think a thorough spanking would help to drive the lesson home. Stand up and come over here."

Nick, having mentally prepared himself for the final onslaught on his completely unprotected bottom, and the smarting, stinging, and burning buttocks it would produce, now had to face a different kind of torment. He rose to his feet and faced his disciplinarian.

Jennifer continued with her explanation. "Some people who are into adult discipline start a session with a spanking as a sort of warm-up, before the caning proper. I never do that. I think a caning is most effective when it's delivered cold, as it were. After all, a headmaster of old would not give his pupils any warm up before caning them, so neither do I. Spankings are very effective, nevertheless, especially when applied to already sore cheeks."

Hearing this, Nick thought his cock would explode. He kept frantically wanting to rub it, but knew he was not allowed. Meanwhile, Amanda was really enjoying the whole scene that Jennifer was creating.

Jennifer sat down on an upright chair and motioned Nick to go over her knee. The spanking that followed literally echoed around the room. Dozens of slaps, delivered on top of the stripes already caused by the cane had Nick struggling to keep still. His initial yelps soon turned into yells as Jennifer smacked merrily away, faster and faster, harder and harder, covering every single inch of the hairy masculine buttocks in front of her, and paying particular attention to the softest parts low down, and right IN the crack.

Finally, when Jennifer was satisfied with the brilliant, bright red, glow she had produced all over every part of Nick' very appealing butt, she told the misbehaving man to get up.

Struggling to his feet, and with his face now blushing as red as his bum cheeks, Nick looked very contrite.

"Ready for the next bit?" Jennifer enquired, not that Nick had any option in the matter.

"Yes, Miss."

"Get back over the table and get that beautiful bottom right UP in the air."

"Yes, Miss."

"Do you accept that you need this?"

"Yes, Miss."

"And do you accept that these next six strokes will be the most challenging for you to take?"

Nick could only agree. However, something in him made him push his bottom up and out a little more, as he took in the significance of this remark.

"There are two, if not three reasons why these coming strokes will hurt quite a lot more. See if you can tell us what they are. See if you can think of three good reasons why your bottom is shortly going to be absolutely on fire with blazing pain."

Nick blushed bright red as he struggled to speak. What he said came out in a sort of strangled whisper.

"Erm, I'm not sure Miss."

"The first reason you can think of?" Jennifer was not going to be diverted from her train of thought. Her inquiry was insistent.

"Because my bum is now bare, Miss."

"Absolutely. There's now no protection for those attractive, soft cheeks of yours. And the second reason?"

"Because my arse is already sore, Miss, and I guess these strokes will be landing on already sore areas."

"You guess correctly, young man. And I will make sure I cane the sorest parts of your buttocks, which will be easy as I can now see them so clearly."

"So can I," put in Amanda enthusiastically. "You've got a very appealing arse anyway, my darling. You know that's what I think, but now you've got some really attractive stripes across it as well."

"Quite," Jennifer agreed. Turning back to the twitching, nervous young man, who was now virtually quaking in fear, she asked "And the third reason?"

Nick couldn't think. In the position he was in, it was hard to think of anything at all except his completely humiliating exposure, and the anticipation of what was shortly to happen to his already heavily punished arse.

He couldn't think of another reason. He remained silent. His partner, Amanda, happily suggested the answer.

"I know the third reason", she said triumphantly. "Because you'll be caning harder. These will be harder strokes."

"You've got it!" Jennifer concurred. "I always make the final six of any punishment the most memorable of all. Much the best way, don't you think?"

Amanda enthusiastically agreed. She couldn't wait to see the effect this last six strokes would have on her handsome lover.

Nick was so shocked, he gasped out loud. He just could not believe what he had just heard. He went deep red. Jennifer swished the cane menacingly through the air a few more times, and a heavy silence suddenly fell across the room.

Amanda leaned back in her chair, looked hard at Nick and then at Jennifer. "Are you telling me that you have not given him really hard strokes already?"

"Oh yes," Jennifer grinned. "All my canings are hard, but these last strokes will be harder still. What used to be known as severe."

At this Nick' mouth just fell open. "Jennifer, I can't … I mean … I can't … we can't do this … I mean …"

He was cut short by Jennifer. "You heard what I said lad. Stick that arse of yours UP, and we'll start again from where we left off."

Nick was so completely stunned, but Jennifer was so commanding. Nick's bare bum and legs were fully exposed to, and within easy reach of that cruel cane. He felt Jennifer's hand rubbing across his cheeks and down the tops of his legs.

"I'm always comprehensive in the punishments I deliver. By the time I've finished with you, young man, you'll have received a very sound caning indeed, but I am definitely impressed with the way you're taking it."

"Thank you, Miss."

"Of course, this should only be seen as a preliminary instalment. I think Amanda indicated you are to be caned like this regularly, until the credit card debt is paid off in full. Are we agreed?"

Nick' eyes grew wider in unbelief at what he had just heard. There he was, bent over, bare arse up, being caned by this older woman, who discussed with Amanda how he was to be further punished. He felt so incredibly small and totally humiliated which, of course, was exactly what Jennifer had intended.

The next ten minutes passed in something of a bewildering daze for Nick. Jennifer took her time. She was going to make sure she could thoroughly enjoy herself.

"Right lad." She tapped Nick's bum with the tip of the cane. "Legs straight, lift your arse up, and keep it up. If I have to tell you that again I will use the cane on your hands."

She then started to quickly flick the tip of the whippy cane all over Nick's arse, with little sharp whipping strokes, the intensity getting stronger with each tap. The cane began to gain a life of its own. Then she started right in Nick's crack and on his hole. Nick clenched his butt cheeks in an attempt to protect his poor exposed most private parts. Jennifer's reaction was swift, the cane was brought down sharply between Nick's cheeks, hitting his hole and just missing his cock. Nick leapt and yelped.

"DON'T clench your cheeks", came the instant command. "Keep your bum relaxed. That way the strokes can penetrate as deeply as possible."

The pain was awful, but there was nothing for it but to resume the position, keep his arse up and spread his cheeks wide open again. He was rewarded with a few even sharper whacks on his bum hole. The pain was increasing, he was squirming even more, and his arse felt as if it had been stung a thousand times. After what seemed like an age, Jennifer stopped. Nick had broken out in a sweat, and was now gasping in shallow breaths.

"Right lad," said Jennifer, "I will now take the cane PROPERLY to your arse. I don't want you jumping about, so keep still, and keep correctly presenting your bottom. I want to get a good aim across your backside because, as I said, these final six strokes will be HARD."

Nick stayed in position, stretched tight over the table. All the flicking and tapping, all the crack caning, it had all been merely a preliminary for the last part of his punishment, the six really hard, severe strokes which were still to come. He was acutely aware that his arse was so painfully and vulnerably exposed.

Jennifer had a practice tap or two on the lower part of his bum.

"You will count each one and thank me for it. Begin."

THWHACK!

"Ow! Argh! One Miss. Thank you, Miss."

A little lower and a little harder still. THWHACK!

"Owwwww! No! Please! Er, I mean, two Miss, thank you, Miss."

And so it continued, each superb stroke delivered harder and lower. By stroke number five Nick was sweating and in intense pain. His arse was smarting like never before, and like it would NEVER recover. He was breathing heavily and pressing completely into the table. He tightened his grip as he felt Jennifer tapping again. Oh no! He couldn't believe what he was feeling. The pliant cane was tapping more and more urgently across the tops of his legs. Something told him that to have the backs of your legs caned would be even more painful than having your bottom punished.

There was a short pause while Jennifer ran her hand across Nick's well-striped bum, giving it a little pinch and a slap or two. Then she resumed the tapping across the tops of his legs.

Deep emotion had now begun.

 "Oh, I am so sorry, Amanda. I am so sorry. Please forgive me. Please, I can't take any more. Please......"

Then it happened.

THWHACK!

"AAAAAAAAAAAAAA ... aaaaaaaaaa ...
ARGH! OW! ... OW! ... OOOOOWWWWWW!"

There was a long pause, during which no one said anything. Then Nick was told to get up. He stood there shaking, his legs weak. Jennifer spoke.

"I think you still have something to say to me, young man."

"Oh, yes! Er, I mean, six Miss. Thank you, Miss.!"

"Good man."

Nick was the one who now had more to say. "Thank you very much for caning me, Miss. And spanking me, Miss. Thank you VERY much indeed."

The discipline had achieved the desired effect. Nick was certainly well punished, very contrite and apologetic, but also VERY aroused. Although the caning had certainly been hard, it wasn't hard enough to cause any real damage. The stripes would be there for several days, but Nick would enjoy viewing them in the mirror each morning, watching them fade until they would be just about completely gone when it was time for his next caning the following Friday. What a perfect punishment. And what perfect stimulus for the really hot times he and Amanda would undoubtedly enjoy together each day. Something inside Nick told him that their love life was going to be taken to new levels not seen before!

Jennifer had yet another instruction, once again delivered completely calmly.

"Right, you can now go and stand in the corner, your nose pressed against the wall, and your hands on your head."

Without a word, Nick did as he was told.

"Stay in the corner. Keep your hands on your head. Think about what you're learning from my excellent cane."

Nick just had to stand there and wait for further commands. More than anything, he wanted to rub his throbbing buttocks, but of course, that wasn't possible with his hands on his head. As he stood there, his bum cheeks clenched tightly and then relaxed. The marks soon started to turn into raised wheals, angry red lines that would be very difficult to forget, and very difficult to sit upon in the short term. Nick – and Amanda also – would greatly enjoy feeling them in the days ahead. A badge of honour!

Jennifer was enthusiastic as she spoke.

"So … how do you feel now about your first caning? And the first of many, I hope."

"Very grateful, Miss."

"Just about the best punishment there is for most crimes. And ideal for any adult age. It will hurt equally as much whether you're 22 or 62, and the humiliation is about the same, I would say, at any age as well. It's very easy to administer, once you've mastered the technique properly, and another advantage is it's so easily available. I know several couples who keep their cane hanging on a hook, prominently displayed either in the kitchen or the lounge. It's then a good, permanent reminder that it's a disciplined household, and it's always instantly available to give a painful reminder to behave!"

Like her now very contrite partner, Amanda was also learning a lot, but in different ways. As a young woman, she hadn't grown up with the threat of the cane hanging over her as someone like Jennifer's brother would have done. She could certainly see the many benefits of caning, and couldn't wait to get started in bringing it into her relationship with Nick. Would it be used one way only? In other words, would it always be for her to use it on Nick if it was needed to drive a message home? Or would they both consensually agree that either of them could, whenever appropriate, instruct the other one to bend over for the intense, all-consuming sting that only a rattan cane could produce?

"Want another drink?" Amanda enquired of Jennifer as she gently laid the cane down on the table where Nick had been writhing and shouting only a few minutes earlier.

Leaving Nick standing, nose pressed into the corner, hands on head, the two women enjoyed a couple more sips of white wine.

"Cheers!"

"It's been great," Amanda told Jennifer, as they relaxed on the sofa. "I never would have known how easy it is to get really good results with a cane. Is there anything else I should know?"

"Well, I suppose I could let you into a few more secrets of good discipline," Jennifer ventured. "I mean, he's been really compliant today, mainly, but you may reach a time when he doesn't take what's coming to him so obediently. Then it's useful to have few more tricks up your sleeve, that'll quickly make him toe the line."

"Such as?"

"Oh, extra strokes for any disobedience. Or, of course, going right back to the beginning. I once told a guy in his fifties I would give him three sixes. Three sets of six strokes, trousers, pants, bare. He took the first six across his trousers without too much fuss, other than a few yelps and gasps when I gave him some harder swipes really low down. Anyway, he dropped his trousers for me and bent over again in just his thin white pants, and took a further six. Then he stood up, dropped his pants and bent over again completely naked. His bare arse was a fine sight, I must tell you, and beautifully striped by then."

"So what did he do wrong?" Amanda innocently asked.

"Well, we got through half of his final six. Then when I got to stroke number four, I decided to SLICE the cane really HARD, right into his crease – the area where his bum meets the tops of his legs. You might guess, that's the most sensitive part of a guy's arse."

"Wow! Go on. Please … go on!" Amanda begged excitedly. Neither of them noticed as Nick momentarily stroked his rampant cock before putting his hands quickly back onto the top of his head.

"I'm going to," Jennifer replied. "So, although I say it myself, that stroke was a beauty. It must have STUNG like merry hell. The guy shouted out an obscenity, jumped up, and started literally dancing around the room, clutching at his burning buttocks. I just waited, until he realised I'd expressly said not to get up until I told him."

"So what did you do?"

"That little mistake resulted in my going right back to the beginning, and giving ALL the strokes again from the start. Certainly concentrated his mind, I'm sure!"

"You are the most incredible disciplinarian."

"Thank you." Jennifer beamed with pride. "In the main, I'm only using the kind of techniques my brother's tutors used when he was in the sixth form. I know a few more tasty ideas that always ensure a man obeys – sooner or later. For example, if you've told him to grip the far side of the table firmly with both hands while he's being punished, here's a way to ensure he does just that. If he loses his grip or tries to get up, calmly and firmly tell him that you'll cane his hands if he does it again. Always carry any threat through. In other words, if his hands leave the far side of the table again, even briefly, tell him to stand up and hold out one of his hands. Either one will do, as you're going to be caning both of them. Two or three sharp strokes right across each outstretched palm will get him yelping and probably clasping his hands under his armpits. Then when he's told to resume his position, bottom up, properly displayed and presented, he'll find it really difficult to grip the far side of the table with hands that are burning and stinging like hell."

Nick's cock was nearly ready to explode as he thought about this. Wisely, he stayed put where he was.

"Then there's writing lines. In the olden days, you were often set a hundred lines if you misbehaved."

"Oh yes", Amanda had heard of that. "I must learn to behave. That sort of thing?"

"Exactly. Except, I make it a lot more interesting than that. If you're coming to me for adult discipline, I do the whole thing for real."

"What do you mean?"

"Well, if I set a hundred lines, I'll dictate something like 'I must learn to remember that any misbehavior or disobedience on my part will result in hard spankings or canings which, although they will always be applied with vigour to my bare, meekly presented bottom, will always be greatly beneficial to me.' Try writing that a hundred times, in very neat handwriting that mustn't deteriorate at all, even towards the end."

"Or", said Amanda enthusiastically, with eyes gleaming as she thought aloud," try writing that just after you've had your hands caned!"

"You're getting the idea! Well spoken!"

Nick found this conversation incredibly horny. His cock was even harder now, pressing urgently against the wall, causing a damp patch to appear. He really wanted to stroke it, the more he thought about what Jennifer had just said. For the moment, though, he sensibly left it alone.

"Did your brother ever get his hands caned?" Amanda wanted to know more details. Both women knew Nick was listening to their whole conversation.

"Oh yes. Only the once. It was so painful that he said he determined to make absolutely sure he would never let it happen again. He told me he'd been really badly behaved, and certainly deserved it, though."

"What did he do?"

"He was in a really aggressive mood, apparently. He was in the sixth form, so already an adult aged 18, and he was moaning about having to abide by all the petty rules like time-keeping, essay writing, speaking politely and respectfully to the teachers, obeying the dress code, etc. etc."

"So why did he get his hands caned?"

"He argued with the tutor at first. He told me it was just a discussion, initially, in which they disagreed. Then my brother said he didn't see why he and his fellows should still be subject to corporal punishment now they were adults. The tutor said a good caning never did anyone any harm, and pointed out that it would hurt just as much even when you were 18 or over. My brother finally snapped and told him to fuck off."

"Wow. Not a good idea in view of what he'd just heard."

"Exactly. He had to go out in front of the whole class, hold out each hand in turn and have it swiped – hard - across the palm. Bloody hurt like nothing he'd ever known, he said. He'd had his arse caned a few times – six of the best - and that is unbelievably painful, as we in this room all now know, but he said hand caning was in a different league."

Amanda ruminated for a bit and then spoke aloud.

"Imagine if they still did that today! I guess young thugs would decide to mend their ways pretty sharpish if that was the punishment for mugging, vandalism, graffiti."

"You've got it in one", Jennifer replied. "How different life could be for all of us."

They were both lost for a minute or two in a happy reverie, imagining a society where young women could walk the streets alone without fear, and where we could all enjoy towns and villages without them being defaced by ugly graffiti, which is threatening and encourages more crime.

The they turned to Nick, still standing in the corner, heavily striped buttocks on display, hand on head and … a very stiff cock standing proudly erect, straining for release.

The well-caned guy felt aroused. In fact, he felt more turned on than he'd probably ever been before. The more he thought about what had just happened to him, the more his cock twitched.

"Turn round and come here", Jennifer commanded. "Have you learned your lesson?"

"Oh yes, definitely Miss."

"Good. The first of many, I think we've agreed. Weekly lessons from now on, until the credit card balance is repaid."

Nick's cock twitched even more strongly, while the two women looked keenly at it. Then they looked at each other.

"Life shouldn't be all pain", Jennifer surmised. "There's room for pleasure as well, without a doubt."

She stole a glance at Amanda and saw she was looking at her partner with a real sparkle in her eyes.

Amanda was horny.

Jennifer was horny, and they both wanted some more fun. Jennifer spoke to Nick.

"Come over here and stand in front of us. You know what we want to do, so make sure you do make it last for us. If you please us both sufficiently, you can have your own time of pleasure afterwards – but leave your cock alone for now. Don't touch it at all. WE want it. Remember the cane is just there on the table behind you."

Nick didn't need a second invitation. While Amanda and Jennifer got into a receiving position, with their mouths wide open, he offered his rampant, moist, dripping member for loving, oral attention.

With everyone being as aroused as they were, it didn't take long. Much slurping, sucking and licking ensued and in just a matter of moments, Nick shot his load all over the carpet using his right hand.

All three adults collapsed together, their breathing becoming more and more relaxed, and Nick was the first to speak.

"Thank you," he said. "That discipline was what I needed. I didn't know that until tonight, so thank you for caning me. And thank you for introducing me to it. No one would believe how much it hurts, but all I can say is ... it hurts SO GOOD!"

"I'm glad you understand now. You're just beginning to learn the many benefits of adult discipline. We'll continue your learning at the same time next week."

"Thank you", came the instant reply.

"I'm glad to see you're starting to learn humility as well. There's just one more little thing to deal with today, before we're completely finished."

Nick' expression changed, and he started to rub his sore buttocks more and more frantically as he listened to Jennifer' further remarks.

"You will recall that I said you could have your own time of pleasure AFTERWARDS, meaning AFTER Amanda and I had our pleasure. I distinctly recall saying to leave your cock alone just now."

Nick started to physically quake with fear as he took in the significance of this statement. Surely Jennifer couldn't be intending any further discipline today? Not when he was SO sore, and not when he'd been so COMPLETELY humiliated?

"Leaving your cock alone means just that. Yet you wanked yourself, just momentarily it's true, while we were pouring more wine just now. You thought I didn't notice.I am your new Mistress now. I am ALWAYS in charge, and in particular, I am now in charge of your cock. You needed to have asked my permission to wank, which on this occasion would not have been given."

"I'm sorry. I'm so sorry, really I am. It was just that I was SO horny. I think the caning had made me just about the horniest I've ever been. I needed to touch myself – right then."

Jennifer smiled quite benevolently as she replied.

"Caning always does have that effect on a virile man like yourself. As for the need for relief, that will have to wait in future. Your cock is mine, young man, from now on. You'll only cum when I give permission, and your young partner here can help me achieve that regime. And I'm telling you now, you're not to cum again until AFTER your caning next Friday. I've got a feeling you're going to be pretty horny by then, so that will be an additional part of your discipline regime."

Nick was now looking down at his feet, blushing bright red.

"Amanda can supervise your cock on my behalf, and we'll keep your lack of relief on that basis for now. From after your caning next week, however, you'll wear a chastity device during the week that will physically

PREVENT you playing with yourself. I mean business when I provide discipline, young man. Now get yourself back over that table, raise your bottom nice and high, and grip the far side with both hands. These six extra strokes are for cumming without permission. Ready? Keep that bottom right UP!"

THE END

(If you're interested in adult male chastity, there are several other Mark Maguire stories featuring this topic.)

Additional bonus discipline story …

Taking It HARD!

Jonathan worked in IT for Outreach Marketing. He had little enthusiasm for his work and found his days at the office quite boring. That was, until everything changed at a business conference, he was sent to which involved a few days away at a big hotel.

The conference brought about a chance encounter that changed his life – for the better!

After returning home from the trip, almost daily, Jonathan would ask himself how he could have got into something so horny, yet something that virtually no young man his age could possibly know anything about.

It had all started that time when he was away from home on that fateful business trip. Jonathan's firm, Outreach Marketing, had sent him away on a training course at a hotel in Derby. In the evening, during free time, he'd found himself with an attractive young woman standing side by side at the bar, waiting to be served. As an inexperienced young man, Jonathan was more nervous than most of the other delegates. He wasn't at all sure this was the best scenario in which to reveal his lack of experience. Everyone else seemed SO sure of themselves, particularly the women!

"You on the same course?" came the question.

"Yeah." Jonathan's reply was minimal to say the least. He looked into the woman's eyes. She was maybe about 40, very feminine, very pretty, dark hair which tumbled over her shoulders, and a neat, coordinated outfit.

"Your first time here?"

"Yeah." Then, after a pause, Jonathan added, "You?"

"It's not my first time at this conference, or at this hotel," came the reply. My dad was at school here in Derby, at Maplestone House.

It's on the edge of town, sits in its own grounds. Got vivid memories of the tales he used to ell me about his time there! Boarding school, you see. He was there in the sixth form."

Jonathan was intrigued. There was something about the way she spoke that was starting to turn him on.

"What sort of memories do you mean?" he enquired.

"Painful."

"Painful?"

"Painful memories. Very painful, according to my dad, but very good memories overall."

"You're losing me here", Jonathan countered. "Painful but good? What are you talking about?"

"I'm talking about the discipline he had in the sixth form. They were all over 18, so they were adults in fact, but in those days they were still subject to the cane. The school was run under the rule of the cane."

Jonathan had heard of the cane but didn't know anything about the way the whole discipline regime used to revolve around regular canings for misdemeanors, small or large.

"If it was so painful, why did your dad think it was so good?"

"A caning is more painful than you might imagine, but SO beneficial in so many ways."

Now the woman seemed to be talking in the present, not about what her dad experienced in the past.

"What sort of benefits?"

"You get the feeling of having paid for your misdeed, of having the slate wiped clean. That was, like, the mental benefit, according to my dad. And the physical benefit was the endorphins. A good caning really gets the endorphins flowing!"

Once again, Emily had switched from the past to the present.

"Endorphins?"

"The feelgood factor. You feel fantastic. Really elated. Really 'high', without the need for any drugs."

Jonathan suddenly realised that his companion was now completely talking in the present tense.

"You mean you're doing this NOW? You're not just talking about your dad's memories?"

"Absolutely."

There was quite a long silence while Jonathan took in this information. He realised he was starting to be turned on, as he tentatively asked, "Are you the giver or the taker? I mean are you top or bottom?"

He blushed bright red. He'd given himself away, indicating without a doubt that he was finding the whole subject arousing.

"Always top. Definitely top. Don't worry. I know what you're referring to. I spotted you when I came into the bar. You look just my type. My name's Emily. You?"

"Jonathan."

"I've seen you before, back at the office in the lift, in the car park, in the canteen."

"Right."

The response was minimal. Monosyllabic. The 31-year-old was still treading as carefully as he could, but was more and more intrigued – and definitely aroused! Was this attractive woman really proposing to CANE him?

After a few drinks, and a longer, more detailed conversation, they found that, although they both worked for the same firm, with the office being spread over six floors of the big, impersonal building, they had never met.

Just one hour later, they found themselves in Emily's top floor suite. Emily, being senior to Jonathan, and personally being used to the discipline game, always paid for an upgrade to a penthouse suite when staying at a good hotel like the one they were currently in. This meant she was the only occupant of the whole floor, and therefore any noise produced by the cane strokes or the reaction of the recipient would not be heard by anyone else. Always best to plan ahead!

The lounge area in the luxury suite was well furnished, with a settee very conveniently placed for administering a good, hard caning to a young man draped over one of the arms.

"Right young man. Let's have you over the Chesterfield, bottom up, nicely presented."

Hesitation. Understandable.

"I'm waiting. I haven't got all day."

Jonathan, wearing a smart suit, removed his jacket and approached the settee. Gingerly, he bent himself over the arm nearest to him, the effect of which was to raise his young arse and provocatively stick it up, just begging for the attentions of his new acquaintance's whippy cane.

Emily wasn't going to spank him first. She wasn't into any kind of warmup. She believed that an adult caning should be realistic. A headmaster of old wouldn't have provided any kind of "easing in".

She tapped Jonathan's bum with the tip of the cane, and Jonathan took a deep breath, tightening his grip of the cushion in front of him.

Tap, tap, tap. Nothing more. But the effect was electric. Those taps with the cane! They went on and on, and gradually became harder, more rapid, and more urgent.

The young man was coming to fear them more than the strokes that were to follow. They were so excruciatingly nerve-wracking. He never knew if the tap would immediately be followed by the first of the proper, hard whacks, or if it was just one of many light taps while Emily measured his distance and took aim. Jonathan became more and more concerned. What the hell was Emily doing back there? Admiring a most attractive arse?

Or imagining the throbbing, horizontal welts that she would soon be producing?

Jonathan could almost smell his own nervous sweat, and his mouth went dry with anxiety.

How could he have possibly got himself into this extremely embarrassing, extremely vulnerable position? What if it just hurt TOO much? What if Emily was really intending to hurt him?

Come to think of it, that would be absolutely great, he decided. In fact, the idea of being caned until there were clearly visible tram-lines across his bare buttocks was starting to turn Jonathan on like never before. He wriggled a bit, and raised his bottom a little more, almost as if he was begging "Please cane me!"

How quickly he was getting into the whole mindset of an obedient sub.

Suddenly the tapping was over, and without any warning ...

SWISH.........THWHACK! The first stroke landed. All thoughts of an enjoyable caning went straight out of Jonathan's mind as he tried to process what had just happened to him. The first stripe had positively erupted across his bottom, quite low down, on the part he'd be sitting on – that's if he was ever able to sit again!

He gasped, whimpered a little, clenched his teeth, then …

SWISH...........THWHACK! The second stroke fell, just above the first. God, it hurt!

The young man tensed up, bum cheeks clenched.

"Don't clench your cheeks. Keep your buttocks relaxed for the cane to do its work properly."

Relaxed? Jonathan had been told to keep his bum relaxed! How could he do that when he was feeling so extremely anxious? This was just one of the facets of adult corporal punishment he was coming to understand.

SWISH............THWHACK!

He didn't even hear the 'swish' the next time, all his efforts now being fully engaged in dealing with the raging fire breaking out all across the lower part of his arse.

Then, suddenly, without warning, came three good, lusty strokes in quick succession.

THWHACK! … THWHACK! … THWHACK!

"Oh no………oh please………oh God! … Please, no more! … Please stop! … Ow! Ow! OW! … Oh, God it hurts! … It hurts so much!"

Jonathan was pleading in desperation for his torment to cease.

"How many was that, five, six, seven?"

Emily was quietly, calmly enquiring, while lightly swishing the cane through the air near to her squirming, gasping victim.

In the confusion of the situation, Jonathan had lost count, and in addition, lost all sense of time or where he was. All he could think about was how much his bare, punished arse was throbbing and HURTING. How much he wanted to rub it furiously in what he surely knew would be a completely futile attempt to rub out the pain.

But he didn't. And he didn't move from the wonderfully submissive position he was in. The strangest thing was that he stayed put, bare bottom meekly presented, passively waiting for what might be going to happen next.

It was Emily who spoke.

"Well done, young man. Well taken. That was what was traditionally know as Six of the Best. Six, good, hard strokes, accurately delivered, all beautifully placed across the lower half of your buttocks – as, hopefully we shall now see."

What did she mean? What were they now going to see? Jonathan's mind was racing.

"If you will be good enough to stand, remove your trousers and pants, we can both see the results of my handiwork – SO FAR!"

So far? Was the demonstration not complete? How many more strokes would there be? How could he possibly take it? Jonathan's thoughts were becoming desperate.

"Stand up!"

The command was forceful.

Jonathan struggled to his feet, and immediately started frantic rubbing of his rear, only to hear that this was not permitted.

"No rubbing. Drop your trousers and pants. Quickly now!"

Jonathan obeyed. There was something about the authority of this beautiful woman that was REALLY turning him on. As he fumbled with his zip, he was aware that his cock was beginning to harden. Soon he was standing in his shirt tails and briefs.

"Pants down as well," came the order.

The young man wriggled as he tugged his underpants down to his ankles and stepped out of them.

"Place your clothes on the upright chair over there and then come back to me."

When Jonathan meekly returned to stand in front of his tormentor, Emily lifted his shirt tails.

"Turn around and bend forward. Oh YESS! That's a beautiful sight, although I say it myself. Now, would you like to see as well. Look in that big mirror there. You can see for yourself."

The handsome young man walked nervously over to the mirror, turned round a bit so that he could see as much of his buttocks as he could. The lower half of both cheeks was now decorated with a neat set of six welts. Clear, red stripes all horizontally placed across the part of his buttocks he'd be wanting to sit down on – if he ever could again!

"Professional, don't you think?" Emily enquired, looking quite pleased with herself and also slightly amused.

Jonathan was completely unable to reply. That was, until Emily continued ...

"Some very attractive stripes. But I'm sure we can improve on them!"

Jonathan was dumbstruck. What did she mean? Surely she wasn't going to inflict MORE punishment on his red, very sore bum? Any more cane strokes would be absolute agony, landing as they would across his now extremely sensitive cheeks.

"Normally, the cane would always be given in sixes in the olden days," Emily was explaining. "But sometimes twelve, or even eighteen strokes were needed to make a young man see the error of his ways."

Jonathan gulped, and involuntarily clutched his burning arse.

"However, I think today, as this has been your first introduction to the delights of the cane, just a few more harder strokes will reinforce the message that I am in charge."

Again, silence prevailed as Jonathan took in the enormity of this remark.

"So! When you're ready young man, bend over again, present your bottom as I instructed before, and raise it up nice and high. Then we can continue."

Slowly, Jonathan walked back to the sofa, draped himself over the arm, and pushed his bottom UP. This had the appealing effect, as far as Emily was concerned, of presenting the beautiful stripes to the very best advantage. Jonathan's young, smooth, masculine buttocks were spread more widely open this time.

Emily noticed a clear sign that her new young friend WANTED her to see in between his cheeks. The very attractive, slightly hairy crack clearly showed the young man's pink, puckered arsehole, which Emily felt was just crying out to be fingered.

But, Jonathan's poor bum! There was no getting away from the fact that it had been well caned.

Emily took careful aim. Then ...

THWHACK!

Jonathan couldn't help but cry out, with a yelp, "Aaaghhh!"

THWHACK! THWHACK!

Were those the extras he'd been promised? Or would there be more? Surely no one could be so cruel. Or could they?

"Stand up lad, hands on head."

Was it over? Jonathan was trembling, his legs felt weak, the stripes all over his bum, from the top to the crease of his thighs, seemed to be concentrating together to bring fresh pain. He stumbled, but managed to straighten up, put his hands on his head, realising that his cock and balls were bouncing in front of him.

He didn't look down or worry about being seen, he was just biting his lips, trying to control himself. How did he feel? What an incredible mixture of emotions overwhelmed him.

Jonathan had discovered consensual adult discipline, administered with a thin, supple, extremely painful school-cane applied HARD right across the lower part of his bare buttocks, while he meekly bent over, touching his toes in front of an older woman whom he was quickly coming to adore.

First, there was the burning, smarting pain. Those cane strokes had penetrated deep into his soft, masculine buttocks, but also into his psyche.

Second, he felt extreme humiliation in having had to meekly present his bare bottom for this older woman to punish.

But third, he felt aroused. In fact, he felt more turned on than he'd probably ever been. The more he thought about what had just happened to him, the more his cock twitched. Soon it was standing proudly erect, straining for release.

He stole a glance at Emily and saw she was looking at him with definite lust in her eyes.

Eyes full of....what? Sympathy? Love? Admiration, or just plain unadulterated lust?

Jonathan looked keenly at his tormentor. His trousers looked full. You could clearly see the shape of her breasts beneath the thin, expensive fabric. What did she want?

Emily was definite as to her needs as an adult woman.

"Fetch a clean towel from the bathroom, spread it on the settee, and then get into position."

In just a matter of moments, Jonathan was back. Emily, legs spread wide, was just begging for it. She started removing her clothes.

"Do you want this inside you?" Jonathan enquired, pointing to his rampant cock, while Emily removed her panties.

"You bet!"

"Sure?"

"Never surer!"

A condom and a little lube were all that was needed, and soon the young man was deep inside his curvy companion. His thrusting started slowly, but quickly became more and more urgent. Emily became more and more aroused as she spread her legs WIDE and greedily TOOK all that her new friend could offer.

This first giving of himself to this wonderful woman was sadly, soon over. Both were gagging for it in their different ways. Jonathan wanted to fuck, Emily wanted to be taken.

As soon as Jonathan was aware that his newfound lover was climaxing, he himself shot his load. He rapidly withdrew and removed the condom carefully.

Both adults collapsed together. They hugged and kissed, their breathing became more and more relaxed, and this time Jonathan was the first to speak.

"Thank you," he said, with feeling. "That was what I needed. I definitely needed to fuck, but I needed the caning as well. I didn't know that until tonight, so thank you for caning me. And thank you for introducing me to it. No one would believe how much it hurts, but all I can say is ... it hurts SO GOOD!"

Emily was a woman of few words. Nevertheless, she had now decided it would be easy, and very enjoyable, to schedule a weekly meeting where they could explore erotic discipline more and more deeply.

"Want some more?" she said quietly.

"Absolutely!" came the immediate reply.

"You're starting to discover the many benefits of consensual adult discipline. So, how about a weekly appointment at my place, after work on a Friday?"

"Oh, yes please!" Jonathan could barely hide his enthusiasm.

"Or ... how about some more RIGHT NOW?"

THE END

Discover the wide range of exciting adult discipline stories by Mark Maguire, featuring man-to-man (gay) and FemDom titles, all available in both paperback and Kindle ebook versions.

Other books and eBooks by Mark Maguire

Caning the Teacher

Six of the Best GAY Discipline Stories

College Canings

Connect with Mark Maguire

website: markmaguirebooks.co.uk

email: info@markmaguirebooks.co.uk

amazon: Search 'Mark Maguire'

About Mark Maguire:

All Mark's stories are fiction and are for over 18s only. The scenes of adult corporal punishment are so graphic that you sense he must be writing from personal experience, which he is!

Mark lives in deepest Dorset, UK and Mistress (Melissa) Jade lives nearby.

Mark tells us "I really enjoy writing about adult discipline, whether Fem-Dom, man-to-man, man to woman or gay. I hope you find my books are as pleasurable to read as they are to create".

Mark knows his subject through and through, and this enables him to really "get inside the minds" of the participants in the stories. As you read, you can choose characters to identify with, understanding exactly how they are feeling.

Mark Maguire can make the descriptions of the spankings and canings so vivid because he writes after many years of actual participation in adult erotic discipline. Enjoy it with him as you read and imagine it's you yourself taking part!

Collect all Mark's books and enjoy them again and again. Write to Mark with your comments on stories you've read and/or give him your suggestions for future titles.

Printed in Great Britain
by Amazon